Copyright © 2004 by Nord-Süd Verlag AG, Gossau Zürich, Switzerland
First published in Switzerland under the title *Onno, das fröhliche Ferkel*.
English translation copyright © 2004 by North-South Books Inc., New York
All rights reserved. No part of this book may be reproduced or utilized in any form
or by any means, electronic or mechanical, including photocopying, recording, or any
information storage and retrieval system, without permission in writing from the publisher.

First published in the United States, Great Britain, Canada, Australia, and New Zealand in 2004
by North-South Books, an imprint of Nord-Süd Verlag AG, Gossau Zürich, Switzerland.
Distributed in the United States by North-South Books Inc., New York.

Library of Congress Cataloging-in-Publication Data is available.
A CIP catalogue record for this book is available from The British Library.
ISBN 0-7358-1937-8 (trade edition)
1 3 5 7 9 HC 10 8 6 4 2
ISBN 0-7358-1938-6 (library edition)
1 3 5 7 9 LE 10 8 6 4 2
Printed in Belgium

For more information about our books,
and the authors and artists who create them,
visit our web site: www.northsouth.com

Hans de Beer
Oh No, Ono!

Translated by Marianne Martens

North-South Books

New York · London

Ono was a very curious piglet. While his brothers and sisters napped or wallowed in the mud, Ono went looking for adventure.

Mother Sow never worried too much about her little Ono for she knew he'd always be home in time for the next meal.

One morning Ono woke up early. Was someone coming?

"I'll catch you, you silly rabbit," shouted Ono, racing after the bunny.

Into the burrow went the rabbit.

Into the burrow went Ono.

Oh no, Ono!

Ono squealed for help, and luckily his mother heard him.

"Oh my silly little piglet," she said, sending him to the mud pool to cool off.

Ono wondered if his tail would ever curl again.

"Five little ducks went out one day, over the hills and far away," sang Mother Duck.

Ono watched the ducklings march across the barnyard.

"Come along babies, hop in the water where you belong," said Mother Duck.

Ono wanted to play with the ducklings.

"Watch out, here comes Super Duckie!" he shouted, making a big cannonball jump into the water.

Oh no, Ono!

All the ducklings were splashed high in the air.

Mother Duck was very angry. "Go away, Ono. You are scaring my babies!"

But the ducklings weren't scared at all!

Ono went to the pasture.

"Ha-ha, ha-ha," he called to the foal, "I may have short legs, but no one is faster than I am!"

Then Ono raced madly around the foal.

The foal was so dizzy watching Ono that he fell down.

"What good are your long legs if you can't use them for running?" teased Ono.

The foal's mother was angry. "I'll show you one use for a horse's long legs," she said and kicked Ono across the pasture.

Oh no, Ono!

Then the foal showed Ono just how fast he could run with his long legs.

Ono was exhausted from all the running. He snuggled down to rest in the hay.

"Stop, thief!" cried the hen. "Help! He's stolen my egg!"

Ono woke with a start, raced out of the barn, and crashed right into the fox!

Oh no, Ono!

But what luck! The egg flew through the air and landed safely on a nest of hay.

"Thank you, Ono!" said the hen happily. "You're a hero."

Ono wasn't quite sure what he'd done, but he was happy to be called a hero.

Ono looked around. He was bored.

I know, he thought, I'll scare the sparrows. He sneaked up behind them and, "Boo!" he shouted.

The sparrows scattered in a panic.

"Ha, ha," said Ono, "I startled you, didn't I?"

Then Ono saw some crows.

I'll scare them, too, thought Ono.

He crept up quietly, then leaped into the air. "Boo!" he shouted.

But the crows didn't move.

Oh no, Ono!

The crows weren't scared. They fought back!

"Crows are very different from sparrows," said Ono.

Ono was hungry.

He saw a tree filled with juicy pears.

"Mmm–mmmm," said Ono.

He stretched and jumped, but he couldn't reach the pears.

Suddenly, a squirrel leaped up into the tree and started eating a pear.

What a good idea, thought Ono.

He took a running start and leaped.

Oh no, Ono!

He smashed into the tree with a thud!

Down fell the squirrel and down fell lots of juicy pears.

Ono apologized to the squirrel, and the two shared the juicy pears.

Ono strolled through a clearing in the forest. Something rustled.

"Who's there?"

It was a little boar. "Ha, ha, ha! What silly stripes you have," teased Ono.

The little boar ran into the bushes.

A great big mother boar ran out of the bushes.

Oh no, Ono! Run for your life!

Ono ran—right through a big mud puddle.

Now Ono had silly stripes, too.

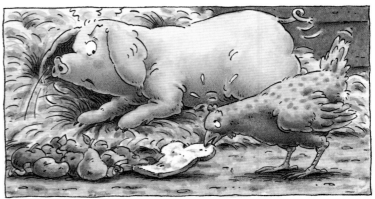

Ono was taking a nap in the barn. Something woke him.

A chicken was pecking at Ono's lunch.

"I'll get you!" cried Ono and chased the chicken all the way back to the hen house.

The ladder bent a little.

Then stretched a lot.

Oh no, Ono!

Up he flew, then down he fell, landing in a prickly bush.

"Are you all right?" asked the chicken. Then she invited Ono into the hen house.

But would he make it out again?

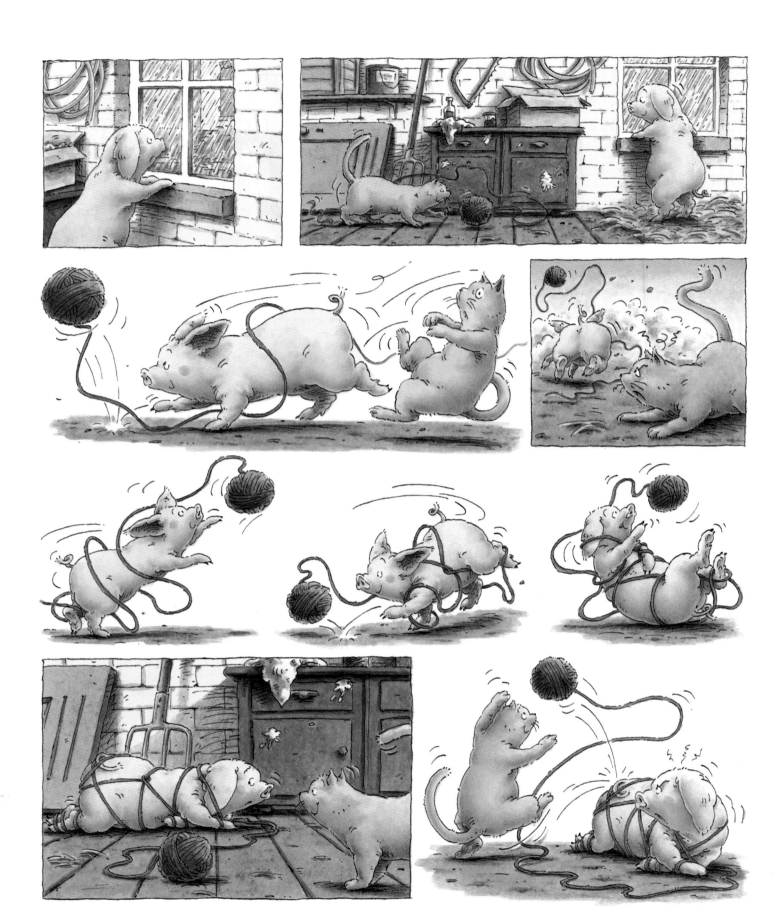

It was raining so Ono was trapped inside the barn. He was bored.

He saw the cat playing with a ball.

"Give me that ball!" cried Ono.

He snapped at the ball. He chased after it. He hopped and twisted and before he knew it, he was all tangled up.

Oh no, Ono!

Then it was the cat's turn to have some fun.

The rain ended, but now Ono and the cat were trapped by a ball of yarn.

Ono hopped happily across the hay field.

What fun! he thought as one by one, he knocked over the haystacks.

"That's the biggest haystack of all!" said Ono and raced toward it.

Oh no, Ono!

He hadn't seen the cow napping behind the haystack.

"I'm sorry," said Ono as the cow shook herself out of the hay.

The cow just laughed. "It looks like you have some horns, too," she said.

Ono's busy day was done. Tired and dirty, he snuggled down to sleep.

"I can't wait for tomorrow's adventures," he said.

Good night, Ono!